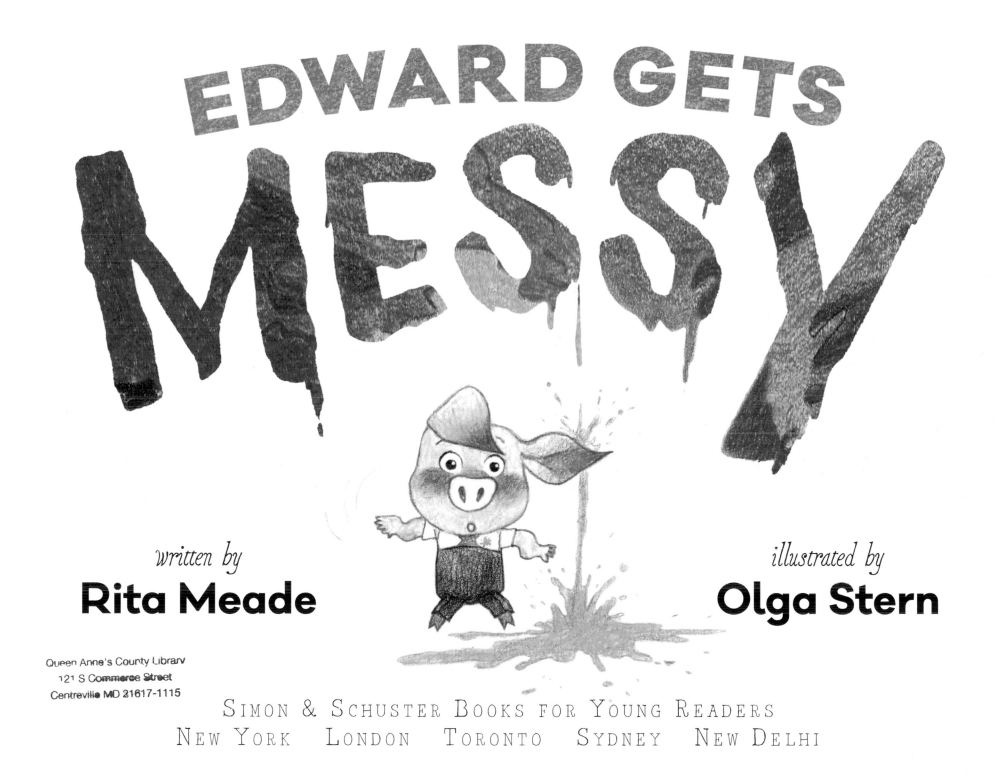

EDWARD GETS MESSY

written by
Rita Meade

illustrated by
Olga Stern

SIMON & SCHUSTER BOOKS FOR YOUNG READERS
NEW YORK   LONDON   TORONTO   SYDNEY   NEW DELHI

For my parents, Virginia and John.
Thank you for letting me get messy.
—R. M.

To my loving family, Igor, Ludmila, and Maria Stern,
for your motivating critique and your endless support
—O. S.

9/16

SIMON & SCHUSTER BOOKS FOR YOUNG READERS
An imprint of Simon & Schuster Children's Publishing Division
1230 Avenue of the Americas, New York, New York 10020
Text copyright © 2016 by Rita Meade
Illustrations copyright © 2016 by Olga Stern
SIMON & SCHUSTER BOOKS FOR YOUNG READERS is a trademark of Simon & Schuster, Inc.
For information about special discounts for bulk purchases, please contact Simon & Schuster Special Sales at 1-866-506-1949
or business@simonandschuster.com.
The Simon & Schuster Speakers Bureau can bring authors to your live event. For more information or to book an event,
contact the Simon & Schuster Speakers Bureau at 1-866-248-3049 or visit our website at www.simonspeakers.com.
Book design by Lucy Ruth Cummins
The text for this book was set in Slimtype.
The illustrations for this book were rendered in colored pencil.
Manufactured in China
0616 SCP
First Edition
2 4 6 8 10 9 7 5 3 1
Library of Congress Cataloging-in-Publication Data
Names: Meade, Rita, author.
Title: Edward gets messy / Rita Meade.
Description: First edition. | New York : Simon & Schuster Books for Young Readers, [2016] | Summary: Wearing his perfectly
clean suit and living in his perfectly tidy room, Edward the pig avoids getting messy until a big tub of paint falls on his head.
Identifiers: LCCN 2015035671| ISBN 9781481437776 (hardcover) | ISBN 9781481437783 (eBook)
Subjects: | CYAC: Cleanliness—Fiction. | Pigs—Fiction.
Classification: LCC PZ7.1.M465 Ed 2016 | DDC [E]—dc23 LC record available at http://lccn.loc.gov/2015035671

This is Edward.

Edward is a very particular pig.

He detests dirt.

He FEARS filth.

He likes things to be just so.

Edward never gets messy.

Each morning before school,
Edward irons his perfectly clean clothes.

He tidies his
perfectly tidy
room until there's
not a speck
of dust in sight.

He vacuums his perfectly sparkling goldfish tank
with a special underwater vacuum.

Edward is very happy with being very clean.
But it's hard work to stay that way.

Edward never pets
friendly dogs on the street.

He never,
ever eats food
that spills or
splatters.

And he never, ever, EVER uses markers or glue sticks or paint.

They are just
too messy.

It sure isn't easy being a particular pig.

On the way to school one morning,
Edward's friends jump in a big pile of dirty leaves.

CRUNCH

But Edward doesn't get messy.

He walks on the sidewalk.

In Edward's science class, the baking soda volcano erupts into a spraying flow.

BOOM

But Edward doesn't get messy. He sits at the back of the room.

At lunchtime, everyone else at Edward's table

eats spaghetti and meatballs.

But Edward doesn't get messy. He eats a plate of steamed broccoli.

On the muddy field outside,
Edward's classmates play a game of baseball.

SQUISH

But Edward doesn't get messy. He stays in the stands.

GLOOP

Edward has stayed clean for most of the day.

Now there's just one class left.

The art teacher gives out paper and paint.

Once again, Edward doesn't get messy.

He straightens up the supply shelf.

But something goes wrong.

To his surprise . . . and his horror . . .
and through no fault of his own . . .

Edward is distraught. Edward is

Edward doesn't
know what to do.

But wait.

The next day at school, Edward helps the
science teacher with her experiment.

Out on the muddy
baseball field,

Edward gets a hit and
slides into second base.

And on the way home from school,
he jumps into that big pile of leaves.

Edward is no longer afraid to
pet friendly dogs on the street.

Or eat food that spills and splatters.

And he happily uses markers
and glue sticks and
ESPECIALLY paint.

Because now Edward knows that it's okay even
for particular pigs to get messy. . . .

After all, they can always clean up afterward.